Withdrawn from Collection
Per CA Ed Code 60510

D0021931

PALO VERDE SCHOOL LIBRARY
PALO ALTO PUBLIC SCHOOLS

Hey, New Kid!

Also by Betsy Duffey

PALO VERDE SCHOOL LIBRARY
PALO ALTO PUBLIC SCHOOLS

Hey, New Kid!

by Betsy Duffey

illustrated by Ellen Thompson

F
Duf

Viking

For Ben

VIKING
Published by the Penguin Group
Penguin Books USA Inc., 375 Hudson Street, New York, New York 10014, U.S.A.
Penguin Books Ltd, 27 Wrights Lane, London W8 5TZ, England
Penguin Books Australia Ltd, Ringwood, Victoria, Australia
Penguin Books Canada Ltd, 10 Alcorn Avenue, Toronto, Ontario, Canada M4V 3B2
Penguin Books (N.Z.) Ltd, 182-190 Wairau Road, Auckland 10, New Zealand

Penguin Books Ltd, Registered Offices: Harmondsworth, Middlesex, England

First published in 1996 by Viking, a division of Penguin Books USA Inc.

1 3 5 7 9 10 8 6 4 2

Text copyright © Betsy Duffey, 1996
Illustrations copyright © Ellen Thompson, 1996
All rights reserved

LIBRARY OF CONGRESS CATALOGING-IN-PUBLICATION DATA
Duffey, Betsy.
Hey, new kid! / by Betsy Duffey; illustrated by Ellen Thompson.   p.   cm.
Summary : Third-grader Cody dreads going to a new school when his family moves,
so he decides to reinvent himself, hoping his new classmates will be impressed.
ISBN 0-670-86760-8
[1. Schools—Fiction. 2. Moving, Household—Fiction. 3. Friendship—Fiction.]
I. Thompson, Ellen (Ellen M.), ill. II. Title.
PZ7.D876He 1996 [Fic]—dc20   95-46309   CIP   AC

Printed in U.S.A.
Set in Plantin

Without limiting the rights under copyright reserved above, no part of this
publication may be reproduced, stored in or introduced into a retrieval system,
or transmitted, in any form or by any means (electronic, mechanical,
photocopying, recording or otherwise), without the prior written permission
of both the copyright owner and the above publisher of this book.

Contents

Chapter 1

Super Cody

"Is your fly zipped?"

Cody's mother looked over from behind the steering wheel of their blue station wagon.

Cody zipped his pants.

"Tuck in your shirt."

"I don't feel so good," he said. He saw a school-crossing sign out the window, and his stomach tightened.

Cody pulled down the car's sun visor and looked in the mirror. "Maybe I'm sick," he said hopefully. "Look at these spots. I think I have chicken pox."

"Cody, keep your imagination under control. Those are freckles."

His mother stopped at a stop sign. "You do not have chicken pox. You just don't want to go to school."

She drove on.

"The first day is always the hardest. You'll be just fine."

"I don't see any parking places," said Cody. "Let's try again tomorrow. Or next week."

A red Jeep pulled out right in front of the school.

"Oh, good," his mother said. "Here's one."

The school was a tall red-brick building with lots of windows. It did not look at all like his old school. To Cody, it looked more like a prison. He imagined that he was a prisoner being driven to jail.

"Don't I get a last request, Warden?" he said to his mother.

She swung into the parking place. "Don't

be silly. Be yourself. By the end of the day you'll have lots of new friends. You'll love this school."

Small groups of kids were walking toward the building. They laughed and talked.

Cody wondered what his friends Aaron and Kate were doing. If he were still in Topeka, he would be with them, making them laugh. School was fun with Aaron and Kate.

One whole week last month they'd pretended to be from another planet. They'd talked like robots and walked like robots. Everyone had laughed, even his teacher.

Another time they pretended to be able to read the teacher's mind. They got out their lunch boxes and lined up for lunch before she called them. And once they pretended that the cafeteria was haunted. Why else would the meat loaf have that greenish color?

Right now, back in Topeka, Kate and

Aaron were walking into his old school, laughing and talking like these kids—these strangers.

"You told me never to speak to strangers. That's what those are, Mom."

She sighed. "Cody, you're hopeless. I give you permission, just for today, to speak to strangers. Come on."

He didn't move.

"I promise it will be fine."

She was already out of the car.

"My legs, Mom. I can't move my legs."

She opened the car door and looked down at him. "There is nothing wrong with your legs."

Slowly he got out of the car and began limping toward the red-brick building.

"I really should stay home. I mean, you might need me, Mom. You'll be all alone," he said to her back.

"I'll be fine. I'll have Pal to keep me company." She kept walking.

"But Pal's a dog. He can't help you unpack. Mom . . ."

She didn't respond, only held the door open for him. As they walked together to the office, he had that prisoner feeling again.

"Hi. I'm Susan Michaels and this is Cody. We just moved from Topeka," she said to the lady at the office window.

The lady leaned out the window and looked at him. "Second grade?" she asked.

"Third," his mother answered. Cody stood up straighter.

"Welcome to Danville School," the lady said. "Come on in, Mrs. Michaels. We have some papers for you to fill out. Cody can sit in the hall on the bench."

Cody sat down alone and clutched his book bag.

Inside was all his new stuff. His missed his old stuff—his chewed pencils, his notebook covered with his drawings.

His mother had not been able to find his

school things in the moving boxes yesterday, so they'd had to buy everything new.

The pencils came in a pack that said NEW! and IMPROVED! The notebook-paper pack said SUPER! and DELUXE!

A girl passed him in the hall. She wore a purple T-shirt and had lots of curly red hair. She was the only person he had ever seen who had more freckles than he did.

She smiled at him. At least he thought she smiled at him. Maybe she didn't smile at him. He looked down quickly.

Who would want to be friends with him anyway?

He was just plain old Cody who was too short and too freckled, whose father worked in a bank and whose mother sold computers. His family drove an ordinary station wagon and had an ordinary cocker spaniel who did nothing but sleep. Boring.

He thought about his new pencils and paper, and wished that he could be NEW! IMPROVED! SUPER! or DELUXE!

"It's another new kid," a boy said to his friend as they passed Cody in the hall.

Watching the boys walk down the hall, Cody wished with all his might that he was not just another new kid. Then, as he waited for his mother, he had an idea.

No one knew him here. He could be anything that he wanted to be. He would no longer be the plain old Cody. He would be a new version of himself, like the pencils and notebook paper. He could use his imagination to make a new Cody. For once his pretending would not be for fun—it would be for survival.

Super Cody.

His mother came out and gave him a hug. "Ms. Mallet will be right out to take you to your new classroom."

She straightened his shirt, then rubbed his cheek with spit.

"Remember what your dad told you this morning," she said, "about the little engine that could. 'I think I can. I think I can.'"

"Mom, I'm not a baby."

"I know, Cody. I just want you to think positive."

"I think I positively don't want to be here."

"Cody," she said, "the kids will love you."

Ms. Mallet came out of the office. Cody gave one more pleading look at his mother before he turned and walked down the hall.

"And remember, be yourself," his mother called to him.

Which is one thing he had decided not to be.

One SUPER! DELUXE! new kid coming up!

Chapter 2

The Little Dork
That Couldn't

"This is our new student, Cody Michaels."

Cody was standing in front of his new class with his new teacher, Ms. Harvey.

A classroom full of strangers looked back. His heart was beating fast—faster, he was sure, than it ever had before. He imagined again that he was a prisoner. Twenty pairs of eyes were fixed on him like the guns of a firing squad. The girl with the purple T-shirt, he noticed, sat in the front row.

"Tell us something about yourself, Cody," Ms. Harvey said. "Where are you from?"

He rubbed his hands together to stop them

from shaking. Topeka sounded so boring. It was time to create the new Cody. "Alaska," he said instead. "We lived in an igloo."

"My," his teacher said.

The twenty pairs of eyes widened. Now he had their attention. He felt a ripple of excitement—like the kind he felt when he made a goal at soccer. They believed him. He took a deep breath, tucked his hands down into his pockets, and continued.

"And I am smart, super smart. In fact a genius."

He stood up taller. Everything was going great.

"As a baby my first word was *encyclopedia.*"

Ms. Harvey blinked. "Tell us about your family."

He thought for a second. His family was boring too. But not for long.

"My dad works for the F.B.I. He's a secret agent."

"Oh!" Ms. Harvey said.

"My mom drives a red Jag."

"Cool," said a boy in the back.

Being Super Cody was terrific. He was in control. He could have anything. He could be anything.

"With black leather seats," he added. "And a fax machine."

"Well," said Ms. Harvey. She paused, then asked, "Any pets?"

"Just Pal," Cody answered, then remembered that he was Super Cody now.

"And what is Pal?"

"He's a . . ." Cody thought hard. Pal couldn't be just a dog. Everyone had a dog. "He's an emu."

Someone gasped.

Cody wondered what an emu was.

"Well," Ms. Harvey said, "I think that's enough for now."

"It is?" Cody was just getting started. "I could tell you about my house and my room." He was thinking about inventing a swimming pool and Ping-Pong table.

"Maybe later," said Ms. Harvey. She led him to a seat right behind the freckled girl in the purple T-shirt.

"Welcome. Have a seat behind Holly."

Cody sat in his new desk and looked around at his new class. His heart was not pounding quite so hard now. His hands had stopped shaking.

"Hey, new kid," the boy behind him whispered.

"It's Cody," he whispered back.

"Can you bring your emu tomorrow?"

"No," Cody answered. "He's shy."

"No talking, Chip." Ms. Harvey looked in their direction. "We start the day with science."

She handed Cody a science book. It was the same one that they had used at his old school.

"We're starting a new unit today," she said. "Chapter twelve. Plants."

"Ooo! Ooo!" Cody—that is, Super Cody—

waved his hand in the air.

"Yes?"

"I just wanted you to know," he said, "that I am an expert on plants. We just finished this unit at my old school."

"Thank you, Cody," she said, "for sharing that."

"I mean, if you need any help . . ."

"I'll keep that in mind."

Cody opened his book to chapter twelve.

The pictures of the leaves and flowers were comforting.

When they had finished chapter twelve, Ms. Harvey showed them a stack of paper cups and a bag of potting soil. "We're going to plant some seeds today," she said.

"Ooo! Ooo!" Cody waved his hand again but this time Ms. Harvey did not seem to see him.

Row by row, the kids went to the table in the back of the room to plant their seeds. Cody kept waving his hand for Ms. Harvey to call on him, but she didn't notice.

Finally it was his turn. He walked back to the table with the kids in his row.

Chip passed out the cups. They scooped dirt into the cups from the bag of soil.

"Hey, new kid," Chip said, "here's your seed."

Cody pressed his seed into the dirt in his cup. It gave him a hopeful feeling to plant the seed. He carefully patted the dark moist soil over it.

"Hey, Holly," Chip said.

Holly was patting down the soil on top of her seed.

"Yes?"

"What are you going to get for your birthday?"

"Rollerblades," she answered.

"Cool! I can skate backwards," Chip said.

Holly's eyes were a wonderful greenish color. Super Cody spoke up. "I'm probably the best skater in the whole school," Cody said. "Maybe even the world."

Holly's green eyes got wide. The way she looked at him made him feel great. He was sorry for a second that he couldn't really skate.

"I've won a lot of skating trophies," he added. "Dozens."

"Wow," she said.

"I can give you skating lessons," Cody said.

"Let's finish up," Ms. Harvey said, "and get to our seats."

Cody smoothed out the black soil on the top of his cup. He put the cup on the windowsill with the others.

"Time for math," Ms. Harvey said.

Cody got out one of his new pencils. He took out his new pencil sharpener and began to twist the pencil in the sharpener. He was good at math. He thought about raising his hand to tell Ms. Harvey how good he was at math.

"Multiplication."

Cody stopped sharpening his pencil. He

wouldn't need it after all. They had not had the times tables yet at his old school.

Ms. Harvey handed out the sheets of problems. Cody looked at the problems, then glanced around the room. All the other kids were writing. They were filling in the answers.

Cody began to write down numbers:

122. 45. 600.

He wrote anything just to look like he knew the answers.

They finished the test and began to pass their papers to the front of the room. Cody passed his paper up.

The new deluxe Cody was getting complicated.

He was from Alaska.

He had lived in an igloo.

His father was an F.B.I. agent.

His mother drove a red Jag.

His pet was a shy emu.

He had won trophies for skating.

And he was smart, super smart.

Cody suddenly wished those things were true.

At his old school, he *was* smart. He made good grades. He didn't have to skate. Here everything was different. Being the new Cody was hard.

He thought about that little engine climbing up the mountain. The happy face of the engine had always irritated him. Then he imagined a large bomb dropping from the sky and blowing up the little engine.

Instead of the little engine that could, Cody had become the little dork that couldn't.

Chapter 3

Die, Die Again

Cody's room at home looked like a tornado had hit it. Boxes were piled everywhere. Some were open, with things falling out. Others were still taped shut.

"Ah ha! Underwear!" Cody's mother pulled handfuls of his clothes out of a moving box. She was acting like unpacking was a treasure hunt.

Cody stood in the doorway. "I'm home," he said.

The room had teddy-bear wallpaper. The teddy bears marched around the walls playing little horns and drums. A baby had lived in this room before they moved in.

Cody leaned against the door frame. He imagined himself as a soldier returning from war. He felt as tired and worn out as if he had just crawled through a mine field.

His mother didn't notice. "Tell me all about school," she said cheerfully, pulling a pile of jeans out of the box.

"Terrible. Horrible."

He staggered over to the pieces of his bed and collapsed on the mattress where Pal lay sleeping. Pal didn't even move.

"Pal doesn't care that I just had the worst day of my life," he said. Pal's tail thumped twice.

His mother stopped unpacking the box and looked at him. "I know it's not easy to move," she said.

"It's easy for you," he said. "Now you don't even have to work."

"It's not easy for any of us, Cody. I miss my job and it's even hard for your dad. He's got to start over at a new bank where he doesn't know anyone either."

"But he wanted to move. He wanted the new job. I didn't."

She sighed. "School couldn't have been that bad," she said.

"You don't know."

"Can't you think of one good thing about the day?"

He thought for a minute.

"Well, an alligator didn't eat me."

She smiled. "I'm so glad," she said. "Anything else?"

"I didn't get abducted by aliens."

"Good," she said. "Want to help me unpack?"

Cody got up and nodded yes. He chose a box and began to pull things out of it. His old life was everywhere.

It was like he was an archeologist on a dig. He could look in the box and tell a lot about himself. He pulled out a baseball glove. *This boy liked baseball,* he thought. He pulled out a drawing pad. *This boy liked to draw.*

At the bottom was a card that his class had given him when he moved. It had all their class pictures pasted on it to form the letters B Y E. *This boy had friends.*

He looked at all the pictures. He had known most of the kids since preschool.

He remembered when Kate had got new underwear in kindergarten and brought it in for show-and-tell.

He remembered when Aaron had dressed up like Pippi Longstocking for a book report. He had even worn a dress.

He didn't know why those silly things made him like them even more.

Cody missed his old friends. It was kind of funny, though, how he missed the little things the most. Like how Aaron and Kate always saved the catsup packets with him at lunch and later they would squash them on the playground and pretend that it was blood.

And he missed their confetti collection. They had been saving all the holes from Ms. Harrison's hole punch. On the last day of school they were going to have a parade and throw them into the air. Now he would not be there to throw the confetti.

Here it was like he was invisible. All the wonderful things that he had told those kids hadn't helped. No one had noticed him all day.

Cody put the card down and held out his arms in front of him. "Do I look a little pale, Mom?" he asked. "I think I'm turning invisible."

"You are not invisible," his mother said. "I can see you just fine."

"I must have been invisible, because no one sat with me at lunch. And no one talked to me at recess."

She walked over and put her arms around him.

"It just takes time, Cody."

"How much time?" he said. He imagined himself as an old man hobbling on a walker into the lunchroom alone.

"I'll tell you what," she said in a too-bright voice. "When your father gets home, we'll order pizza. They have a Pappa's Pizza here just like in Topeka. Your favorite."

She gave him one more hug.

"Then we'll talk about school. Your dad can give you some tips about being a new kid. He moved three times when he was young."

She walked back to her box. Cody sighed.

There were a lot a good things about his dad. He always had time to play ball or help with homework. But he was not good at giving advice. It seemed like he always talked in sayings like "Waste not, want not." Or "A stitch in time saves nine."

Cody could never figure out what his father meant. Usually he just pretended to agree.

He watched his mom unpacking the box.

His parents were usually so concerned about him. That's why he couldn't understand why they had ruined his whole life just for a new job.

"Ah ha!" she cried. "Socks!"

She pulled out two handfuls from the box.

His father's car horn honked outside.

"There's your dad," his mother said. "I'm going to order that pizza now." They hurried downstairs.

His dad came through the door, dropped his briefcase, and held out his arms to hug Cody's mother.

"There's no place like home," he said to the mess around him.

His mother laughed. Cody didn't.

"Cody has the new-school blues," said his mother.

"Well, son," his father said, "tomorrow is the first day of the rest of your life. Remember, if at first you don't succeed, try, try again."

Cody thought of his own saying. If at first you don't succeed, *die, die* again.

Pizza was usually his favorite food. But tonight he was not one bit hungry.

PALO VERDE SCHOOL LIBRARY
PALO ALTO PUBLIC SCHOOLS

Chapter 4

Smiley Faces

The next morning Cody checked his cup of dirt and imagined that he was a world-famous gardener. He would grow a wonderful plant—a beautiful, healthy flower.

"Grow!" he commanded, but nothing happened.

The soil was still smooth and black. He felt sad for the little seed alone under the dirt.

"It takes time," said Ms. Harvey.

"How much time?" he asked.

"Time enough."

"Are you sure that it's okay under there?"

29

"I'm sure," said Ms. Harvey. "Take your seat. Time for math."

"Hey, new kid." Chip leaned over Cody's shoulder and looked at his math test. "You got a *zero!*"

Cody stared at his paper. Beside the zero it said *See me!*

Chip leaned closer. "I thought you said you were super smart. Like your first word was *encyclopedia.*"

"I *am* smart." Cody thought for a second, and then Super Cody answered, "It's not a zero. See, it's a smiley face." He drew in two dots for the eyes and a big smile.

Chip giggled.

"Right," he said. "Ms. Harvey always gives smiley faces when you miss all the problems."

Cody looked at the row of Xs down the side of his paper.

"X stands for *excellent,*" he said.

"You're funny," Chip said.

Cody looked at his paper and felt sick.

He had never gotten a zero before. The new improved Super Cody was turning out all wrong.

Why couldn't he just tell Chip that he hadn't learned the times tables yet?

Cody was quiet while Ms. Harvey went over the math tests.

Chip tapped his back. "Hey, new kid."

"It's Cody."

"Can I come and see your emu after school?"

"Not today," Cody said.

"Why not?"

"He's at the vet."

"What's the matter with him?"

Cody tried to think. He remembered when Pal had cut his foot and they had taken him to the vet.

"Oh, he's got a hurt paw."

"Paw?"

The way Chip said the word *paw* made Cody wonder. *Does an emu have paws?*

"Time for social studies," Ms. Harvey said.

They made time lines of their lives. Cody was glad they didn't have to show them to each other. He was sure his was the shortest one:

born   lived   became a new kid,
                   happily   life over

0 1 2 3 4 5 6 7 8 9

years

In English they wrote about their favorite people. He wrote about Aaron and Kate and the confetti collection. But halfway through the story his nose started to run, and he had to stop.

"Lunchtime," Ms. Harvey called out.

Kids began to get their lunch boxes and money. They picked up their jackets for recess after lunch.

A boy stopped by Cody's desk.

"Hey, new kid," he said. "I'm assigned to

eat with you so you won't have to eat alone again."

He made it sound like Cody was some kind of class project. *Do your math. Write a story for English. Eat with the new kid.*

Cody got up and walked beside the boy.

"I saw you get out of a blue station wagon this morning," the boy said.

"So?"

"So I thought you said your mom drove a Jag."

He had to think fast. "The Jag is in the shop."

"Sure. How come if you're from Alaska the license plate said Kansas?"

Cody didn't answer.

It was all getting too complicated. People didn't seem to like the new Cody very much.

The boy looked at Cody's lunch box. "So what do people from Alaska eat for lunch?" he asked. "Blubber?"

Some kids in line laughed.

Cody felt sick.

"I forgot something," he said.

He dropped back to the end of the line. He imagined that he was a prisoner who had just escaped from a chain gang. He had to get away.

He passed Holly, but he didn't look up.

"Hey, new kid," he heard Chip say, but he didn't answer. When the kids in his class turned to the right to go to the lunchroom, he turned to the left.

He didn't care where he ended up, as long as it was not the lunchroom.

He saw a door marked BOYS and went inside. He was a prisoner again—this time hiding out from the enemy.

He hid in the bathroom stall and thought.

He had to make Super Cody even more super, more deluxe, more wonderful.

He waited, thinking hard, until he heard the end-of-lunch bell ring.

Then he went back to class.

Chapter 5

Mom-asaurus

"Mother's Day is Sunday," Ms. Harvey said. "Write a story about your mother and later in art we'll illustrate the stories."

Cody got out a sheet of notebook paper. He looked at the paper and thought about his mother. What should he write?

My mother has brown hair.

My mother sells computers.

My mother likes to unpack boxes.

His mother, he realized, was boring.

A plain old mother.

He wished his mother was a spy, or an astronaut, or an American Gladiator . . .

36

Why not?

He thought about the Gladiators on TV. They all had names like Ice or Dragon or Tiger.

He needed a ferocious name—like a dinosaur.

He began to write.

Mom-asaurus

My mother, otherwise known as Mom-asaurus, is an American Gladiator. She is one of the strongest women on earth. Her hugs can be fatal.

When he read his story to the class, not one mouth was closed.

"Well," Ms. Harvey said. "That was quite interesting."

She didn't say anything after the other kids finished reading their stories. No one, Cody was pleased to notice, had a mother as exciting as his.

"Time for art," Ms. Harvey said.

The kids lined up.

"Where are we going?" asked Cody.

"To the art room," said Chip.

They didn't have an art room at Cody's old school. They had an art cart.

Cody loved the art room. It was a sunny room with long tables. In the center of each table was a cluster of baby-food jars filled with paint. A brush waited at each place.

"Oh boy," said Holly. "We get to paint."

She turned to Cody. "Do you like art?"

"I love art," he said. It was the first truthful thing that he had told about himself.

"Me too," said Holly.

He sat by Chip. Holly sat across from him.

They painted with the brushes.

Holly painted her mother in a white dress. Her mother was a nurse.

Chip painted his mother wearing blue jeans and a T-shirt. She was holding plants. She liked to work in their vegetable garden.

Cody painted his mother in her Gladiator costume.

"I need brown," Holly said. "For the patient's bed."

Cody showed her how to mix the red and blue and yellow paints together to make brown.

Music played while they painted. For one whole hour Cody forgot that he was a new kid.

"Can I come over after school?" Chip asked as they walked back to Ms. Harvey's room.

Cody stopped.

He really wanted Chip to come over, but how could he say yes? He couldn't let Chip meet his mother or Pal. And there were teddy bears marching around his room!

"My mom's still unpacking," he said. "I can't have friends over."

"You want to come to my house?"

Cody was filled with joy, like a balloon that had fresh air blown into it.

"Sure!" he said.

"We can stop by your house and ask your

mom," Chip said. "I want to see your mom, anyway. Does she have her costume at home?"

The balloon popped.

He shook his head.

"I shouldn't play today. I have to unpack."

When Cody came back into the room there was a white envelope on his desk. On the front of the envelope it said NEW KID.

Holly turned around. "I'm sorry," she said. "I couldn't remember your name."

"Cody."

"It's for my birthday party Saturday. Everyone in the class is invited."

She smiled at him. At least he thought she smiled at him. He wasn't sure. Maybe she didn't smile at him. He looked down.

Cody took the envelope and put it in his pocket. He smiled. He had been invited to a party!

He waited until no one was watching and then he opened it. On the front of the invitation was a giant roller skate.

Come to a skating party! the invitation said.

Cody's heart sank. He remembered his words from yesterday. *I've won a lot of skating trophies. Dozens.*

He wished that he had never started being Super Cody. Chip and Holly seemed to like him, but who did they like? Cody or Super Cody? How could he ever know for sure?

The bell rang for them to go home.

"Cody?" Ms. Harvey came up beside him. "I have something for you."

She handed him a small rectangular box. "Flash cards," she said.

"Oh." Cody took the box. It was one more painful reminder of the things that he could not do.

"Work on them at home with your parents. I'm not going to count your math grades for a while."

"Thanks." Cody stood up and went to the table at the back of the room. He wanted to check his paper cup one last time before he left. The dirt was still smooth. No sign of life.

"Ms. Harvey?"

"Yes, Cody."

"Do you think it's going to be okay?" He was still looking at the paper cup. "My seed, I mean."

"Yes," Ms. Harvey replied gently. "It just takes time, Cody."

"How much time do you think it will take?"

"Oh," she said, smiling, "time enough."

How much is enough? Cody wondered.

Chapter 6

To Skate or
Not to Skate

"Ah ha! Spoons!"

His mother was in the kitchen, unpacking. The floor was covered with crumpled paper. Pal was sleeping next to one of the boxes.

"So how was your second day of school?"

"I lived," Cody answered.

He stepped over the piles of paper and sat down on a kitchen stool. He rubbed Pal's back with his foot.

"Good," she said.

Cody pulled the invitation out of his pocket.

"Mom," he said, "I can't go to a skating party on Saturday, can I?"

She looked up from the box and smiled a big smile.

"Of course you can."

"I can?"

"I knew you would get along just fine here." She was beaming. "You're already invited to a party."

"Everyone in the class was invited, Mom. It's no big deal."

"I'm just glad you want to go."

"You'd better not let me. I might get hurt."

"It'll be fun."

"I might break a leg, or an arm, or my gallbladder."

She leaned down to the bottom of the box. Cody could only see her legs.

"It could be dangerous," he called to the legs.

"Ah ha!" she said. "Steak knives."

"Never mind," Cody said. He stood up.

"Wait," she said as she put the steak knives into a drawer. "I have two surprises for you."

She led Cody to his room.

"*Ta da!*" she said. "I finished your room today."

His bed was put together and made up with his baseball bedspread. All the boxes were gone and his clothes were put away. His baseball glove and ball were on one shelf, his art supplies on another. It made him glad to see his things, but it made him sad, too. The room looked so permanent. Like he was really here to stay.

"The second surprise," she said, handing him a brown envelope. "It's from Aaron."

Cody's heart lifted at the sight of the envelope.

After his mother left he opened it.

Inside was a cassette tape. Cody went over to his stereo and put in the tape. Like magic,

Aaron's voice came over the speakers.

"Helllllloooooo!" he said in one long burp.

"Greetings from the planet Topeka."

Cody sat back and listened.

Aaron had made the whole tape as if he were living in outer space. Cody closed his eyes and listened to Aaron's voice, pretending that he was with Aaron. He smiled the whole time he listened.

It made him feel good to know that somewhere, there was still someone who knew him. Really knew him.

He wanted to write a letter to Aaron but he didn't know what to say. He could tell Aaron that everything was great. That he was cool and popular here.

But somehow he couldn't do that. Aaron liked the real Cody.

Cody got out a piece of paper and began to write. He told Aaron about the times tables and the skating party. After he finished the letter he illustrated it.

He drew a picture of a boy in front of a

firing squad. And one of a boy hiding in the boys' bathroom. And finally, on a blank piece of paper he wrote *The Invisible Boy*. He put the letter in an envelope and wrote Aaron's address on the outside. After he wrote *Topeka*, he put his pencil down. Topeka was far away. Aaron and Kate were there and he was alone.

He spent the rest of the afternoon helping his mother. He didn't want to stay in his room by himself.

After dinner he worked on the flashcards with his father.

"Two times two?"

"Four," Cody answered.

"Great," his dad said. "Practice makes perfect."

Cody had already learned that anything times one is always the same number. And anything times zero is always zero.

They practiced until bedtime. "Remember, Cody," his father said as he tucked Cody into bed, "to be or not to be—that is the question."

Cody lay in bed and tried to fall asleep. He couldn't. He could only think about school.

He tried to count sheep, but he could only imagine teddy bears marching around his room.

He tried to count the teddy bears, and he could only imagine them on roller skates.

Another question lingered in his mind. *To skate or not to skate*—that was the *real* question.

Chapter 7

How to Fall

"Nothing!" Cody said in dismay. His soil was still smooth and black. "I don't think it's ever going to grow."

"Come sit down," said Ms. Harvey. "Give it time."

Cody checked his seed three more times that morning.

Once after math.

Once after science.

And once right before lunch.

As he had yesterday, he decided not to go

to the lunchroom. He followed the line of kids, but when they turned right, he again turned left.

He passed the boys' restroom, and continued slowly down the hall. At the end of the hall he saw a door marked MEDIA CENTER. He pushed open the door and went inside.

He could hide with all these shelves of books around. Maybe he could even find out what an emu was.

He looked along the shelves until he found a dictionary.

Emu: A large flightless bird resembling an ostrich.

Cody stared at the words, then closed his eyes. He opened them. He'd hoped that the words would disappear, but they were still there.

His pet was a large flightless bird resembling an ostrich.

He thought of something else. He had told Chip that it had paws. He felt sick.

Cody closed the dictionary. He wished that he could be sitting in the cafeteria with the other kids. He wished he could go to Holly's party. Most of all he wished he had never started being Super Cody.

"Can I help you?" A woman with an armful of books walked up to him. "Where are you supposed to be?"

What should he say? What would Super Cody say? He tried being plain old Cody this time.

"I'm a new kid," he said. "I didn't want to eat lunch by myself."

She stared at him for a moment. "I'm Mrs. Kindress, the media specialist," she said. "You can stay."

"I can?" Cody's breath came out in a loud whoosh. He wished that he could start over and be plain old Cody in his class too. But it was too late there.

"But no eating in here."

"That's okay," Cody said. "I'm not hungry."

"Can I help you find a book?" Mrs. Kindress said.

Cody glanced around at the shelves. He saw a shelf labeled HOW-TO BOOKS. "I need a how-to book," he said.

"How to do what?" she asked.

"How to be a new kid."

She shook her head. "I know we don't have anything like that."

Then he remembered something. "Do you have a book about how to skate?" he asked.

"I think so," she said. "We'll look it up."

She walked over to a computer terminal and typed in *Skating*.

A list of books flickered onto the screen.

"How about this one?" She pointed to a title.

Let's Skate.

Cody nodded.

They quickly found the book. He found a seat and opened up *Let's Skate*. It was filled with pictures of skaters.

54

Some were twirling blurs. Their arms were gracefully curved over their heads.

Some were skating on one foot.

A boy in one picture was leaning forward on one foot with his hand brushing the ground as he skated.

It looked so easy.

There was an entire chapter on the T-position. The T-position was the basic skating stance. You stood with the heel of one foot against the middle of the other foot, forming a T shape.

According to the book, this was the safe way to stand. In T-position your feet could not roll out from under you. That was an important thing to know.

He pushed one foot against the other under the table. That wasn't so hard.

Next he read a chapter titled "Skating Tips."

Take your time.

Find someone to hold your hand.

Always look up, never down.

That was easy! Maybe he could go to Holly's party after all. So what if he'd never skated before? Anything was possible.

He turned the page and frowned.

The chapter was called "How to Fall."

You should not fall with your arms out in front to brace you. The wrist was the most commonly injured body part for skaters.

Cody closed the book. He decided he *would* go to the party and he *would not* fall. Falling could be dangerous.

He thought of the advice that his father had given him once when he had tried out for a baseball team: Nothing ventured, nothing gained.

Then he thought of his own saying: *Nothing ventured, nothing pained.*

He rubbed his wrist all the way back to Ms. Harvey's class.

Tomorrow he would skate.

Chapter 8

How Not to Skate

HAPPY BIRTHDAY HOLLY!

A sign was draped over the entrance to Sparky's Roller Rink.

Cody sat in the car with his present for Holly on his lap. He and his mother had bought the present at the drugstore last night. He had chosen a tablet of drawing paper and a box of markers. He knew that she liked art.

"You sure you don't want me to come in with you?"

"I'm sure, Mom."

"I could stay and watch."

"No thanks."

He opened the door.

"I'll be back at three to pick you up. And Cody, have a great time skating."

Cody swallowed. "Right." He waited a moment before he went through the doorway.

It was dark in Sparky's. Red, blue, and green lights blinked above the wooden floor. Kids from his class circled by, graceful on their skates.

He followed a group of kids to the skate window. He told the man his size and got his skates.

They were heavier than he expected. He spun the wheels. They made a whirring noise and spun for a long time.

Cody found a spot on a bench and took off his tennis shoes.

He put the skates on and pulled the laces tight. He tied the tops in a bow, then a double knot. The brown leather felt stiff against his ankles. He stood and placed his feet carefully in the T-position.

"Hey, new kid!" Chip skated by him. "When are you going to skate?"

"Soon," he answered. Then: "Hey Chip," he began, but Chip was already gone.

Cody looked out at the oval-shaped rink. A chain of girls skated by, holding hands. They snaked around and between the other skaters. He had seen kids play crack-the-whip on the playground. It wasn't so bad for the kids at the front of the chain. But the kid on the end went fast. Too fast. Especially on the curves.

He would not want to do that.

Across the floor he could see Holly. He watched her skate along the back stretch. Her hair was pulled into a ponytail tied with a white ribbon.

His heart pounded a little faster when she whizzed by him.

Whir. Whir. Whir.

Her new Rollerblades whirred to the rhythm of the music.

Clap. Clap. Clap.

She clapped in time to the beat.

Here she came again.

Cody stood up straighter as Holly swooped low around the corner. Her eyes met his.

She smiled at him—or at least he thought she smiled at him. Yes, he was sure that she had smiled at him. Hadn't she?

She had smooth, gliding style that made skating look easy. That was how he would skate.

As he watched the other skaters, he learned quickly how *not* to skate.

Some of the skaters skated *chimp style.* Hunched over. Weight forward. Their arms dangling in front like a chimp, and swinging back and forth as they skated.

He would never make that mistake.

Then there was the *windmill style.* Weight back. Arms rotating in backwards circles, like a windmill.

He would never do that either.

Worst of all was *crab style*. Scooting along flat on your back. Hands on the floor underneath you like a crab.

He would never skate *crab style*.

He would skate smoothly, he hoped. Already he had seen five falls. Five spectacular falls.

One girl sat on the side bench with a Baggie full of ice on her knee.

A small boy sat beside her rubbing his wrist.

The song ended. The beat picked up.

Whir. Whir. Whir.

Clap. Clap. Clap.

The others whirled around the rink.

"Come on!" Chip said.

Cody shifted his feet back just an inch to try to get a feel for the skates. He couldn't put it off any longer.

"Come *on!*"

Cody moved his feet out of T-position.

He bent his knees and arms for balance.

He held his body slightly forward. His heart began to beat faster, in time with the music.

The music changed. Faster now.

"Come on!" said Chip. "I want to see you skate."

"I don't like this song."

"Who cares about the music," said Chip.

"I care . . . You see—"

"Ladies and gentlemen!"

Chip cupped his hands and called out to the other kids on the rink like a ringmaster at the circus.

Cody had to stop him.

"Wait . . . I—"

"Children of all ages!"

"Please . . . not—"

"We now present . . ."

Chip flung his arm to point at Cody.

Cody swallowed hard as every pair of eyes moved in his direction.

"The new kid!"

Chapter 9

Ready, Set, Go!

Ready . . .

Set . . .

Go!

Cody pushed off the rail and rolled forward.

For one second everything was perfect. He glided gracefully. He even managed to smile at Holly as she whizzed by him.

This was easy!

Then his feet began to move. They slipped backwards. They danced forward.

"Eeeeeeeeee!" he screamed.

He skated *windmill style*. Weight back. His arms rotated frantically around and around.

First forward.

Then backwards.

Then forward again.

Cody couldn't catch his balance.

"Way to go!" Chip called. "Cool move."

Chip began to skate *windmill style* too.

"*Eeeeeeeeee!*" Cody screamed again.

"*Eeeeee!*" Chip answered.

Three other boys from his class joined in.

"*Eeeeee!*" they shouted. Their arms rotated like windmills.

"Cool!" one yelled.

"Teach me!" still another boy called out, and joined in.

Cody's windmill turned into the backstroke and his legs kicked like the frog kick he'd learned on the swim team.

"*Ooooooo!*" he screamed.

"*Ooooooo!*" they answered. They all began to frog-kick too.

He started to fall backwards.

He grabbed in front of him. To his horror he imagined himself flat-out on the skating rink.

He yelled to Chip in a moment of pure panic, "Help! I can't skate!"

"What!"

"Help!"

"I'm coming!"

Chip skated forward to help him.

Just then the chain of girls, linked by their hands, zipped by.

"Come on! Crack the whip!" he heard one of the girls call.

He didn't want to fall in front of the girls. Desperately he grabbed in the air—grabbed for anything to keep him upright.

Before Chip could save him, the last girl on the line grasped one of his flailing arms and suddenly he jerked up and rolled forward, the last link in the whip.

He sped along, pulled by the chain.

The kids on the sidelines cheered.

The faces around him became a blur. He saw Holly's face go by. And Chip's.

The longer he held on, the faster he went. There was only one thing he could do. He didn't know what would happen but he had to try something.

He let go.

He braced himself to fall.

But he didn't fall.

He waited to roll to a stop, but he didn't even slow down.

He sailed across the floor.

On one foot.

Then the other.

Back and forth.

Out of control.

He flew over the small curb at the end of the rink.

The crowd parted and watched in stunned silence as he continued on across the expanse of carpet.

He was headed right toward a door, but he couldn't stop.

He put his arms out to brace himself for the crash as he neared the swinging door.

As he pushed it open and flew inside, he saw golden letters on the front.

He could barely read the writing as he whizzed by. The golden letters said:

GIRLS' BATHROOM.

Chapter 10

Boy!

The door slammed shut.

There was silence for a moment, then a high-pitched voice screamed one word:

"Boy!"

Cody had been in some tight spots before. Tight spots were usually his specialty. He could always say just the right thing to save himself. His imagination had never let him down.

Once he had torn his shorts during P.E., when he had jumped off the balance beam and squatted down like he'd seen a man do in the Olympics.

Rip!

His shorts had split in the back. Before anyone could even laugh he had come up with the perfect line.

"Oh good, air conditioning!"

Another time he had burped during quiet reading time. Accidentally, of course. Before he could even get into trouble, he had again said the perfect thing.

"I'm reading about space men," he had said. "That's the way they say 'Good morning.'"

But to roller-skate into a girls' bathroom . . . a girls' bathroom full of girls. For once, there was nothing that he could say.

He closed his eyes. "I'm not look—"

"Eek!"

"Boy!"

Screams echoed around him.

"I didn't mean—"

"Help!"

"There's a boy in here!"

Then the high-pitched voice said:

"Get him!"

Cody put his hands up to protect himself. Rolls of toilet paper hit him from all directions.

Streamers of white toilet paper rained down on him from over the tops of the stalls and from the crowd of girls beside the sink.

"Honest, I'm not look—" A roll hit the top of his head.

He tried to back up, but he couldn't. Instead his skates rolled out from under him and he fell down on the bathroom floor.

The entire room was a snowstorm of toilet paper.

The voice spoke again. This time it called out:

"Wrap him!"

The girls sprang into action. Toilet paper was wrapped around his legs. Toilet paper was wrapped around his middle. Toilet paper was wrapped around his head.

He was a toilet-paper mummy.

Someone put her hands under his elbows

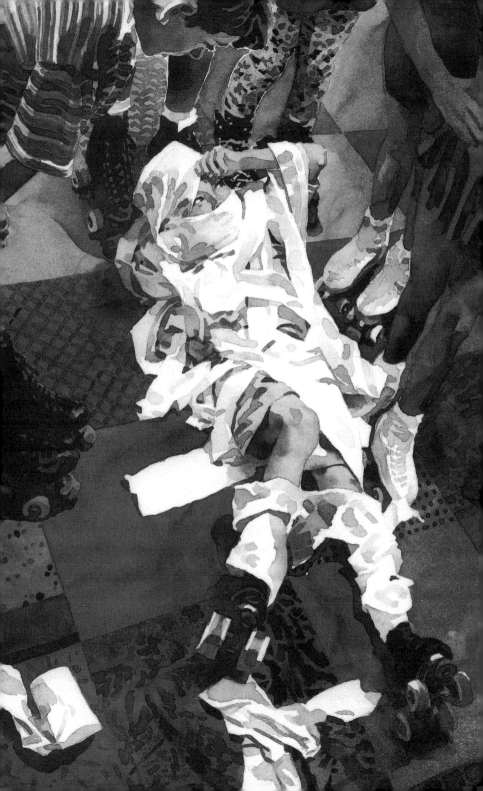

and pulled him to his feet. Somehow he re-
gained his balance. He steadied himself, his
arms reaching blindly, trying to find something to hold him up. Was he going to make
it? Was he going to survive the girls' bathroom?

Hands gave him a push. The door burst
open. And back out the door he rolled.

Cody sailed across the carpet, blinded by
the toilet paper. He couldn't see where he
was headed, and he couldn't stop. His
weight shifted back and forth as he made
his way across the floor.

He felt arms grabbing him, and he sank
down to the carpet. He took a deep breath
and reached up to pull the toilet paper from
around his eyes.

He peeled off one layer. Then another
and another.

He looked around.

There were Chip and Holly and all the
kids from his classroom. Every mouth was
in a perfect circle.

Chapter 11

The Truth?

Cody's brain worked frantically. He had to think up an excuse to get himself out of this one.

What could he say?

He unwrapped a long piece of toilet paper from around his head.

He looked around at the kids. They all stared at him.

He tried to think of a story.

Super Cody would answer like this:

It was my skates.

They were taken over by a magic spell.

Like that story about the red dancing shoes.

Remember? The shoes that kept dancing?

Cody shook his head. That was dumb. That one would never work.

He had another idea. He could say something like this:

I was working on a science project.

It's about moving objects.

You know—action and reaction.

I was testing the force it takes to stop a moving object.

He sighed.

That would never work either.

He looked at Chip. *He* knew the truth— that he, Cody, couldn't skate. Chip had heard him yell it out right before the girls pulled him into the chain.

He took a deep breath. It was time, he decided, to get rid of Super Cody for good.

"I have never been on a pair of skates in my life," he said softly.

"He says he can't skate," someone said.

"He can't really skate," someone else echoed.

"That's right," Cody said, louder. "I can't skate."

He pulled himself onto a bench and began to take off more toilet paper.

As he unwrapped the paper, he talked.

"And we don't have a Jag, we have a station wagon."

He couldn't look up. He pulled white paper from around his arm.

"And I didn't move from Alaska, I moved from Topeka."

Now that he had started, the words came more easily.

"And my dad works for a bank, not the F.B.I."

He unwrapped the other arm.

"Pal is a cocker spaniel, not an emu."

He pulled the rest of the paper from around his chest. "And my first word was not *encyclopedia.*" He took another deep breath. "It was *Mama.*"

He waited for some kind of reaction, but everyone was silent.

"Time for cake!" Holly's mother called from across the room. Cody was afraid to look up. He just stared at the floor until everyone had gone over to the table set up by the concession stand.

He listened as the kids sang "Happy Birthday." The happier they sounded, the worse he felt. He thought about calling his mother to pick him up early. More than anything, he just wanted to be somewhere else. Anywhere but Sparky's Roller Rink.

He looked at the pile of toilet paper at his feet. Super deluxe Cody was gone for good—and he was just a plain old new kid all over again.

Chapter 12

Skating Smiles

Cody listened as Holly opened her presents. He wondered if she liked the drawing pad and markers. He did not go and see.

He cleaned up the scraps of toilet paper on the floor and threw them away. He felt like he was throwing away the pieces of Super Cody one by one, until they were all gone and only Cody was left.

He watched the kids go back onto the rink.

He didn't join them. He sat on a bench and watched them skate.

He decided that he would go into the

mountains and live in a cave, away from all people. He tried to remember what you called someone who did that. A kermit?

"Hey, Cody," Chip called, then skated over beside him and sat down. "Why didn't you come for cake?"

Cody didn't say anything. He stared at his knees instead.

"What's wrong?"

"I think I'm going to find a cave and become a kermit," he said.

Chip smiled. "You mean a hermit," he said.

"Yeah," said Cody. "A hermit."

"Can I come too?" said Chip. "We can live on berries and nuts."

"Or order pizzas," Cody said.

Chip laughed. "You're funny," he said.

"Thanks," Cody said. "I think."

Chip grinned at him. "You know," he said, "you've still got some toilet paper on your face."

Cody put his hand to his forehead. He felt yet another piece of toilet paper and pulled it off of his head.

"I can't believe the way I skated. It was so dumb."

Chip began to laugh again. "It *was* dumb. But it was funny. You should have seen those girls come out of the bathroom," he said. "I'll never forget it."

Cody smiled just a little.

"And the way you took that curve on crack-the-whip. You should have seen your face!"

Cody's smile got bigger.

Chip was laughing so hard now that he couldn't even talk.

"I guess it *was* kind of funny," Cody said. He pulled a piece of toilet paper out of his collar and they laughed together.

Holly skated up.

"What's so funny?" she asked.

Chip was still giggling. "He is," he said.

"We're going to become kermits."

Holly grinned. "You mean hermits." She sat on the bench beside Cody.

"I'm sorry," Cody said. "About the emu and all."

"That's all right," Chip said. "I sort of figured it wasn't true."

"You did?"

"It's kind of a new-kid thing," Holly added. "I know how it feels."

"How would you know?" Cody said to her.

"I was a new kid last year. I told everyone I was a great tap dancer. Everything was fine until recess when they asked me to dance. It was awful."

Chip laughed. "I remember that," he said.

Cody smiled. "I know just how you felt."

Holly got up. "Come skate!" she said.

"No way. You saw what happened last time."

Chip smiled. "Come on," he said. "We'll teach you!"

Chip took one arm. Holly took the other. Cody stood up between them. His skates slipped forward. Then his skates slipped backwards, but he didn't fall down. Holly and Chip held him up.

"Let's go!" Chip said. "This is my favorite song."

Cody grinned. "I like this song too," he said.

They had just learned something about each other. Something true.

The beat picked up.

Cody remembered his skating rules:

Take your time.

Find someone to hold your hand.

Always look up, never down.

Learning to fit in at a new school, he decided, was a lot like learning to skate. The same rules applied. *Take your time.* It took a while to get to know people. *Find someone to hold your hand.* He looked at Holly and Chip and smiled. *Always look up.* He thought of the happy face of the little engine

chugging up the hill. It didn't seem so irritating now.

The lights twinkled brightly. They stood on the side of the rink for a few seconds, watching the other skaters. He looked at Chip and then at Holly.

"Ready?" Holly asked.

"I think I can," he answered.

She smiled at him. At least he thought she smiled at him. Yes, this time he was sure that she had smiled at him. And he smiled back.

Chapter 13

Time Enough!

Ms. Harvey passed back the math tests.

"Hey, Cody!" Chip tapped Cody on the shoulder. "What did you get?"

Cody smiled.

It was nice to hear his name—his real name. He had begun to think he would be called "new kid" forever.

"Eighty-five!" Cody held up his math test for Chip to see.

"Cool!" Chip said.

"Want to come over after school?" Cody asked. It was nice not to worry about Mom-asaurus and a pet emu.

"Sure." Chip nodded.

"Class!" Ms. Harvey said in an excited voice. "Look!" She was standing by the window at the back of the room.

Cody and Holly and Chip and the other kids all ran to the window.

Tiny green plants had pushed their way up out of the soil toward the sun.

Cody found his cup. Three tiny leaves had appeared over the weekend.

"It made it!" Cody said.

Gently he picked up his cup and examined the tiny green stem. It looked pretty strong. He touched it carefully. It sprang back.

He knew what would happen next.

The stem would grow.

Then more leaves would grow.

Finally the plant would flower.

"When will it bloom?" Chip said. "How long?"

"Some things just take time," Ms. Harvey answered.

"But how much time?" Chip asked.

Cody smiled and answered, "Time enough."